Ibn Battuta
AND
THE LOST SHADOW

Copyright © Hood Hood Books

Hood Hood Books
46 Clabon Mews
London SW1X OEH
Tel: 44.171.5847878
Fax: 44.171.2250386

British Library Cataloguing–in–Publication Data
A catalogue record for this book is available from the British Library

ISBN 1 900251 21 3

Origination: Fine Line Graphics -London
Printed by IPH, Egypt

Ibn Battuta

AND

THE LOST SHADOW

Abd al-rahman azzam

Illustrated by Khalid Seydo

The Story So Far ....

In the previous book, *Ibn Battuta Son of the Mighty Eagle*, our hero became so enchanted by some love poetry that he decided heroically to travel to India to find the person for whom the poetry was written. First of all he had to cross the Red Sea with some unlikely companions! Finally, after adventures in Africa, Ibn Battuta found himself in the beautiful city of Muscat in Oman ready to resume his journey. His shadow, however, had made other plans ....

In 1325 Ibn Battuta, a 21 year old scholar and religious judge set off from his hometown in Tangier to perform the pilgrimage. Little did he know that he would not return home for 23 years, and that he would visit lands as far away as China and Timbuktu! Today, Ibn Battuta is recognized as one of the great travellers of the world.

IBN BATTUTA

&

THE LOST SHADOW

Exactly one day before he left Muscat, at midday to be precise, Ibn Battuta discovered what had been troubling him. In the previous week he had been busy making preparations for his departure from Muscat, from where he planned to cross the desert to Mecca and then travel north to Syria and then on to the land of the Turks.

As each day passed, however, he had a nagging feeling that something was missing, that he had forgotten something of profound importance. Although he racked his brains, he could not, for the life of him, figure out what it was.

Not until the day before his departure, as he rushed out

into the midday sun on a last errand, did he discover what had, for the past few days, been missing. This discovery left him dazed, as if he had been struck down by a runaway camel. Ibn Battuta realised that his shadow had disappeared.

In reality he should not have been astonished, for shadows are not what they seem. But to understand this, as to understand anything, one needs to start at the beginning.

A long, long time ago, when the past was still the present and when men could still speak the language of the animals and the birds, there lived a King. As Kings do, he ruled over a Kingdom – which was neither large nor small. As a young man Aramauld – for that was the King's name – had been taught by the land's finest philosophers and trained by its fiercest soldiers. He was greatly loved by his subjects, for he was both brave and wise, generous, but not foolish.

One night Aramauld had the strangest of dreams. He saw himself sitting on his throne, dressed in his finest imperial regalia, down to the ostrich feather sticking out of his crown. Standing next to him in his dream were all his ministers

listening to his wise and sage words, except that they were neither wise nor sage.

"My dear counsellors," Aramauld dreamt himself saying, "we have a shortage of milk in our Kingdom. Now I have given this matter some serious thought. From today onwards all my subjects will eat nothing but grass. Since cows eat grass and produce milk, so shall we!"

At dawn, Aramauld woke up and, smiling, shook his head. "What a peculiar dream!" he thought to himself. However, he stopped smiling when he had the same dream on the second, third, fourth, fifth and sixth nights. On the seventh he did not sleep, but the following night his dream was patiently waiting for him. By this stage, he was getting rather worried. What could it all mean? Was there a hidden meaning? What message was being sent to him? For the time being he told no one, lest people should think he was crazy.

Nevertheless, his ministers could not help but notice that their King appeared perplexed. At first they thought that it was due to the pressure that must bear on anyone wearing the ostrich crown. That all changed at the fateful meeting at the monthly Council of Ministers.

As was the custom, all the ministers were gathered

around the King, each one taking turns to talk about the state of the country. It was while the Minister of War was speaking about military matters and the reform of the army, that Aramauld suddenly interrupted him.

"What is the state of our milk?"

"Sire?" The Minister was perplexed.

 5

"Our milk? What is its state? Is there enough in the land?"

The ministers exchanged dumbfounded glances, puzzled as to what their King was referring to. At that point, the Vizier, who was an old friend of Aramauld, spoke out, "the milk is plentiful, Sire. There is no shortage."

"Excellent," the King sighed with relief, "but tell me, is there enough grass?"

An anxious murmur now spread around the Royal Chamber. What could this mean? Had their beloved King lost his mind?

"The grass is green, Your Majesty," the Vizier reassured him.

"Excellent, excellent." Aramauld now sat back in his throne. "Now what about those army reforms?"

And so a year passed, and the ministers' anxieties faded when they saw that their King's judgements were as wise as they had always been, save for the two perplexing questions which he asked, without fail, at every meeting. As soon as he was reassured that the milk was plentiful and the grass green, the meeting would proceed smoothly.

Then a strange thing happened. One morning, as the

Vizier was reading his reports, he came across an urgent message from the Under-Secretary of Dairies, stating that there had been a drastic fall in the milk reservoirs, and that unless urgent action was taken, there would be no milk for the children of the Kingdom.

The Vizier could not believe his eyes. How could this have happened? Why had no one told him earlier? At once, he dashed out of his office, and, rushing to the Royal Palace, he demanded an urgent meeting with the King. Aramauld was sitting on his throne, and one glance at his friend's anxious face was enough to make him realise the gravity of the situation.

"It is the milk, isn't it?" he asked.

"It is, Your Majesty," replied the Vizier, "but how could you have known all this time?"

Aramauld did not answer, but instead inquired urgently, "What can be done?"

"Well, Sire, we can buy more cows, grow more grass, drink sheep's and goats' milk ..."

"I know what needs to be done," Aramauld interrupted his friend, his voice steady and solemn, "I have known for a long time, but if I tell you, you will think I am crazy."

"Your Majesty, for as long as I have known you, you have spoken nothing but wisdom. Even when we thought you were ..." The Vizier stopped abruptly, embarrased to complete the sentence.

"Crazy?" Aramauld prodded him gently, as he stroked his beard.

"Unusual," replied the Vizier. "Even when we thought you were unusual, I now see how wise you were."

For a while Aramauld remained silent. Then, in a barely audible voice, he mumbled, "The people must eat grass."

"Grass?" spluttered an astonished Vizier.

"Grass." And then the King told his Vizier about the dream which he had had for the past three hundred and seventy nights. The Vizier listened carefully, his mouth open in astonishment.

A spell of silence now gripped the room as both men were lost in their thoughts. The situation was indeed grave, what could this all mean? "There might be another solution," Aramauld's words shattered the silence. "I will abdicate my throne. Perhaps that will please the gods."

"Never!" The Vizier jumped to his feet and rushed to the throne, "never, Sire, never." He, more than anyone else, knew how well Aramauld had served his country. An abdication would surely stir up unrest in the kingdom.

It was at this moment that a guard entered the chamber.

"Your Majesty, an old woman requests to see you."

"Not now," snapped the king, "I have urgent matters to deal with."

The guard shrugged almost imperceptibly, "I will send her away at once, Sire." He began retreating from the chamber, "in any case she is a crazy old woman muttering nonsense about dreams of milk and grass."

"What?" Both the King and the Vizier shouted in one voice, "Send her in at once!"

A few seconds later an ancient-looking woman shuffled in. She appeared to be as old as time (except that in those days time was not very old) and bent over like a banana (except that no one knew what a banana looked like). Her eyes were shiny and black, like two dates (dates, people could understand as they were the national fruit of the Kingdom). When she opened her mouth, one could see that only three teeth had survived the ravages of time, so that they appeared as three stars glittering in the dark universe of her mouth.

"Who are you and how did you know about my dream?" thundered the King, his voice booming off the walls of the Chamber.

"Who I am and how I know is not important," replied the old woman, "what is important is to know what needs to be done."

"And what needs to be done?"

"Your Majesty," the old woman's voice was firm for one so old, "before we get to that, I must ask you one question. Have you not noticed anything missing recently?"

"No, I do not think so," replied the King, checking his clothes, his slippers, and his crown with the ostrich feather. "No, everything is here."

"Would your Majesty mind walking to that window over there and then answering the same question?"

"What impertinence!" The Vizier was on his feet. "Do you not know..."

Aramauld, however, silenced him with a wave of his hand. Deep down he was rather amused, for no one had ever dared to tell him to do anything. And so, he descended from his throne and took the seven steps necessary to reach the window. He then checked himself again, his slippers, his

clothes, his crown. "No, nothing is missing."

"Would Your Majesty mind looking at your feet and then answering?"

Once again the King glanced at his golden slippers. They looked exactly as they did every day (not that kings often examine their feet, they had people for that kind of work). By this stage Aramauld was getting rather impatient, "Look old woman," he bellowed regally, "I told you, nothing is missing."

"Sire, your shadow is missing."

And, you know, she was absolutely right. The King's shadow was nowhere to be seen. Aramauld looked at the ground in amazement. He turned around in a complete circle, he stood on one leg, he looked over his shoulder, he looked between his legs: but there was absolutely no trace of any shadow. "But," he spluttered, "but where has my shadow gone?"

"You have to understand, Your Majesty," replied the old woman, "that shadows are notoriously mischievous. In many ways they are like little children. If you do not discipline them, they will turn out to be very naughty."

"I don't understand," Aramauld scratched his crown in

puzzlement. "I thought that shadows were just shadows."

The old woman smiled gently. "Your Majesty, when God created man, He also created two things to accompany him, man's shadow and his dreams. Both exist because of man, neither can exist without him. During the day the shadow accompanies its owner. At night shadows return to their home – the shadowlands – to rest while the dreams take over. Now, there is normally no problem; but occasionally, as in your case, Sire, the shadows and the dreams may cross paths on their way to work or on their way home to rest. And, as tends to happen, they start to talk. Soon both are complaining about how hard they have to work; the shadows grumble about how agile they need to be, the dreams about how hard it is to be varied and imaginative. At root, both resent being at their owner's constant service. And so, from idle talk, plots are hatched. And that, Sire, is what has happened to you."

"You mean to say that my shadow and my dreams are plotting against me?" Aramauld asked in bewilderment.

"Exactly, Your Majesty."

"How dare they?" he roared, "How dare they? Do they not know who I am? I will declare war on them. I will teach them. I will show them no mercy. I will ..." Aramauld suddenly ceased roaring, realising how ridiculous his words were. After all, how can one declare war on one's own shadow? For a few seconds he was silent, then in a low plaintive voice, he asked "What can I do?"

"Your Majesty," replied the old woman soothingly, "there is no need to worry. For the solution to any problem is to understand it. And you now understand the problem.

All this time the Vizier was standing silently, listening avidly to what was being said. He now spoke: "You mean to say that His Majesty's shadow and his dreams came together and thought up this dream about lack of milk and people eating grass?"

"Exactly."

"But why?"

"I told you, they were childish."

"But there is one thing I do not understand," interjected the King. "If all this was just a dream, how come the milk reservoirs are actually dropping. Who is causing that?"

"An excellent question," answered the old woman. "You see, the plot was very clever. While the dream kept His Majesty occupied, the shadow set about touring the country, ordering the cows to stop producing milk. Since the milk reservoirs were plentiful, it took a year for the shortage to be felt."

"But I do not understand," said the King "how can a shadow order cows to stop producing milk?"

"As Your Majesty well knows, cows are very good-natured, but they are not the brightest of God's creatures. If someone who looks like the King and speaks like the King visits them and orders them to stop producing milk, then they are only too glad to obey."

"But you say that the shadow ordered the cows. Do shadows speak?"

"Speak?" the old woman chuckled, "Speak? Shadows are regular chatterboxes. They would spend the whole day talking if they could. You should hear them. But of course you cannot, as God ordered them to be silent when accompanying their owners. Now shadows may be mischievous and naughty, but not even they would dare go against God's will."

By this stage Aramauld was pacing up and down the chamber, shadowless. His face had turned beetroot red with anger. "So, as far as we know," he fumed, "my accursed shadow could at this very moment be impersonating me

somewhere in the northern province?"

"With your pardon, Sire," interrupted the Vizier, "now is the time for cool reflection." Then, turning to the old woman, he asked: "You said earlier that the solution comes with understanding the problem. We have understood, as far as we can, this extraordinary problem. The question is, how do we get His Majesty's shadow back?"

"Oh, that is the easy part," chuckled the old woman. "As I said, shadows and dreams cannot exist independently. They are destined to follow their owner. They have to, they have no choice. All you have to do, Your Majesty, is remind your shadow who is meant to follow whom."

"Remind him?" The King looked puzzled, "but who knows where my scoundrel of a shadow is?"

"Oh, it doesn't matter where he is, he will hear you. He has to, he is your shadow. He will return, he may sulk for a while, but he will return."

"Very well then," Aramauld huffed, and strode to his throne where he sat himself down. Then, in a loud, regal voice, he ordered his shadow to return. "Now listen here, shadow, I know you can hear me. God has willed that you fol-low me until I reach my grave, and your absence has been noted. I command you to return at once!"

And there he was. Almost as if he had never been away. For a while the King stared fixedly at his shadow. He opened his mouth to scold him, but instead laughed out loud when he saw his shadow opening its mouth in reflection.

"He is back," Aramauld beamed, "my shadow is back." Then, turning to the old woman, he asked: "How can I ever thank you?"

"You can thank me, Your Majesty, by allowing me to leave and by asking no further questions, for there is some knowledge which can only be revealed in Paradise. But remember, Sire, Heaven is watching you, and a King, above all, must be just." With these words, the old woman bowed low and departed, leaving behind King Aramauld, his Vizier and their two shadows.

Silence followed as each man was lost in his thoughts. Both realised that they had witnessed a strange, but miraculous, event. Darkness began to engulf the Royal Chamber as the sun set, and guards entered, bearing candles which they hung from the walls. Soon, the Chamber would be full of the laughter and gaiety of the evening's banquet.

"Do you play chess?" Aramauld broke the silence,

turning to his Vizier.

"Spasmodically," he replied.

"Spasmodically?" The King chuckled. "How can anyone play chess spasmodically?"

"After what we witnessed today, Your Majesty, anything is possible."

King Aramauld laughed out loud and leant back in his large, cushioned throne. Tonight, he reflected, he would get a good night's sleep, the first for a very long time. He might even have a large glass of hot milk before he blew out the candle next to his bed

We left Ibn Battuta in the midday sun. Luckily, he was wearing the magnificent turban which he had bought in Alexandria,[*] and was thus spared certain sun-stroke. It was also fortunate that Ibn Battuta was a learned man. On many occasions over the years he had heard the story of King Aramauld and his mischievous shadow, but had only half-believed it. A fairy-tale he had thought; but even fairy-tales can have their uses.

[*] see *The Travels of Ibn Battuta (Book 1)*

And so, in the Muscat midday sun, once he had recovered from the surprise of being shadowless, Ibn Battuta knew exactly what he had to do.

"SHADOW!" he bellowed at the top of his lungs, nearly scaring to death a passing fisherman. "If you are thinking of returning to your idle shadow-friends in Tangier, then think again! If I choose to travel to Turkey and India, even if I choose to go as far as China, then you will follow. If I change my turban twice a day, then so will you. If I travel on horse-back, then you will need to find a horse. Do you understand? Now, I am leaving Muscat at dawn tomorrow, and I expect you to be here ready to depart."

That night Ibn Battuta had the strangest of dreams. He was back in Tangier, surrounded by his family and friends. In front of him were two tables, the first was groaning under the weight of delicious foods with heavenly aromas, all his favourites. On the other table were piles and piles of beautiful turbans, a galaxy of colours and textures.

Ibn Battuta woke up with a start. It was still a few hours before dawn, and the sky glittered with so many stars, it was as if Heaven had lit up all her candles. Drowsily, he got out of bed and lit a candle which he put in front of his hand.

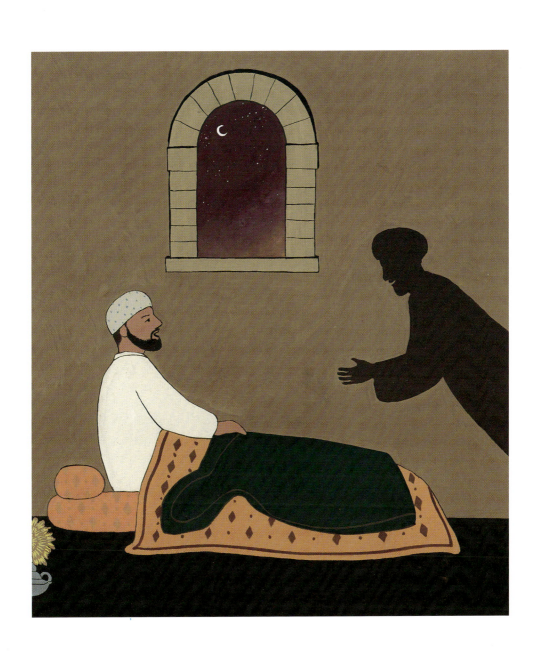

There was still no sign of his shadow. Taking a deep sigh, he blew out the candle. "There are another two hours before dawn, shadow," he hissed, "and do not for a moment think that you and your accomplice, dream, can convince me to return to Tangier. We – myself, you and dream, still have more travelling to do. May Heaven help you if you are not here when I depart!" With these words, Ibn Battuta got back into bed, and went straight to sleep, for he knew that he had a long journey ahead of him. There were no further dreams that night.

At dawn, Ibn Battuta's shadow was waiting for him, and together they set off to resume their travels. Occasionally, if Ibn Battuta glanced out of the corner of his eye, he would swear that he saw his shadow pulling faces at him, or even sticking out his tongue. But he did not mind, and he smiled to himself, for he knew that his shadow would not dare leave him again.

What he could not see was the shadow himself smiling. For deep down (except that shadows are not very deep) he did not really mind being recalled. Over the years he had come to like this young Moroccan. As far as owners went, the shadow reflected, he wasn't too bad at all.

25

THE TRAVELS OF
IBN BATTUTA
SERIES

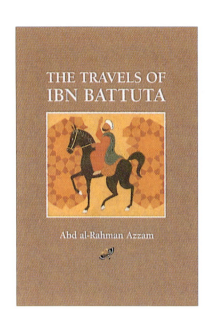

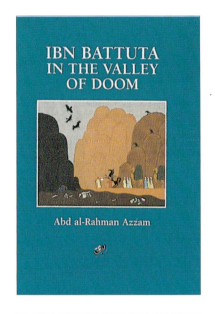

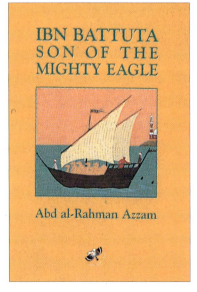

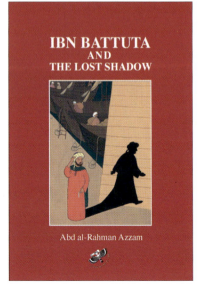